SUSPENSE STORIES V3

GREAT SUSPENSE STORIES

ABDUL RAHIM KHURRAM

Contents

1. Good Neigbours   1

2. He, Who Vanishes   8

3. I Am Death   11

4. I'm Becoming Insane   22

5. I'm Going To Let Go   29

CHAPTER ONE

Good neigbours

Christina was wary of her neighbours.

She lived on a peaceful street in a little town in the middle of nowhere, where you might be excused for believing that people still dropped by their neighbours' houses for a cup of sugar. However, beneath the vertical blinds and carefully manicured hedges, a tangle of secrets and gossip simmered. Nothing in this community, not even Christina herself, could be accepted at face value at an era when keeping one's face was important.

Christina lived on a little street that ended in a cul-de-sac. Christina, who was just 27 years old and had short ringletted brown hair, was by far the youngest of her neighbours. Mrs Johnsons lived just across the street from her unremarkable grey home. Mrs Johnsons was usually out in her yard, caring for flowers, pansies, petunias, and the like, smiling and waving to each passing. Christina had always questioned why she spent so much time in her garden, which was a thriving hive of life. Mrs Johnsons had always reminded her of Mrs Gladys Kravitz from the TV programme 'Bewitched'. At first glance, she appears to be perfectly pleasant, but she is constantly watching, talking about, and reporting on her neighbours. Christina felt the gardening was really a pretext.

The Smiths sat next to Mrs Johnsons. Tom, Silvia, and their two children with golden hair. They reminded Christina of the family from the 1950s 'American Dream' commercials. All that was lacking was a white picket fence. Mr. and Mrs. Ryan lived to Christina's left, retired school teachers who spent countless hours after school instructing different youngsters from the neighbourhood. Christina was intrigued by the constant stream of guests that came and went. Tom, whose home adjoined hers on the right, was the only other neighbour she had really talked with. He had a gigantic Rottweiler that was always barking and drove her insane, which was how they met. Christina rushed up to the door and started beating hard on it. 'Hey, guy, your dog simply won't stop barking. I'm trying to sleep, and he's disturbing the peace and quiet of our whole neighbourhood. "Would you please silence him?"

"Sorry, she's a jittery creature." I apologise for bothering you. I'll bring her inside for a few minutes, okay?" He'd responded quietly.

"Yeah. Ok. Thanks"

"By the way, my name is Tom," he said as he introduced himself.

"Oh, Christina," she said, uncomfortably extending her hand.

"What are you doing attempting to sleep at this hour?" he inquired.

"Oh, I ah... work night shifts," she said, retreating down the stairs and beginning to heel. "I'm sorry, but I really need to get ready for work."

"Well, don't let me keep you waiting; it was lovely to meet you," he had added. "I'm sorry, but I'll deal with Ruby."

Christina and Tom had interacted regularly since then, typically when Ruby had lost her calm and barked as if she had seen a ghost. Christina would have to walk up to him on each time and demand that he do something about that blasted dog. But no matter what Tom tried, he couldn't convince Christina to come inside and have a drink with him.

Christina got up from the sofa and put her head out the window after being jolted back into the present by loud barking. Yes, it was Ruby from next door, acting crazy once again. Christina attempted to ignore the sounds since she was not in the mood to cope with Tom's overly friendly advances, but she was compelled to get up after fifteen minutes of nonstop animal howls. She rang the doorbell as she walked down the stairs, down the curb, and up onto the porch, rocking back and forth. When the door opened, she began her monologue.

"Could you kindly bring Ruby inside, Tom?" She's been going off for the past fifteen minutes-" she came to an abrupt halt as she realised the person at the door was not Tom.

"Who are you?" she inquired. "I'm on the lookout for Tom."

"Well, there isn't any Tom here," the stranger said. "It's just me, Patrick."

"Do you know when Tom is going to return?" she inquired

"I'm sorry, but I don't know any Tom," said the guy. "However, I've just recently purchased the home, so I'm still getting to know my neighbours." "Do you live just next door?"

"Oh yeah, right there," Christina said, pointing to the left. "When did you purchase this house?" she inquired.

"I just acquired it via the family attorney last month," he said. "It seems that this mansion has been embroiled in legal wranglings for the past 10 years, ever since the last owner died in sad circumstances."

"Are you sure?" Christina responded, perplexed.

"Well," he said, looking around. "I'm not sure for sure, but I heard from the attorney that when her husband died, his widow couldn't bear living here anymore, but she couldn't show her right to sell the property since everything was in his name."

Christina was at a loss for words.

"I'm sorry I couldn't be of more assistance, Miss..."

"Christina. "Thank you for your assistance, but no thanks."

"It was a pleasure to meet you."

"You too!" said Christina as she walked back home.

She lay in her bed, the smooth fabric of her nightgown clinging to her thighs. She was happy until a chilly hand stroked her leg. It started reaching up her thigh, pulling up her nightgown and softly exploring at the delicate skin underneath. Gently at first, then quicker and harder in an attempt to reach into her. She glanced up, terrified and petrified, to see who her assailant was, and discovered it was Tom. The plain yet mild-mannered next-door neighbour with the wavy slicked back brown hair, peering hungrily at her from the shadows...

Christina sprang to her feet and climbed to switch on her bedroom light, knocking over a water bottle in her hurry. Water accumulated on the wood, trickling down the drawers and onto the hardwood flooring. Unnoticed, she sank back onto her pillow and glanced at the cheap flower print hanging on the wall opposite her bed in the comforting yellow light. It seemed like a nightmare, she thought. A flashback to the moment when life yanked her out of infancy and into adulthood. One terrifying recollection mingled with another, tormenting her precious hours of slumber. Even the Retoril she took before going to bed couldn't put the horror at bay. Her true tormentor had been imprisoned twenty years before, along with her dreams for a normal upbringing. Christina felt imprisoned in a dreadful limbo of nothingness, too afraid to confront the past and too anxious to face the future. She was aware that they referred to her as a survivor, but she couldn't bring herself to believe it. She felt like a zombie, alive but soulless, moving yet not moving.

Sighing Christina sprang from her bed to get her iPad. She retreated beneath the covers and started looking for her vanished neighbour on the internet. Although she didn't know Tom's last name, she attempted looking for his first name and his address at the same time. After numerous dead leads, she came upon a potential lead in the form of a 2006 obituary. The dates and ages seemed accurate for the neighbour she knew, and they matched the facts the new neighbour had given her. It said:

'Tobey BORIS MAZOKOV'

On May 9th, 2006, at the age of 28 years, he died unexpectedly. Lucy's loving husband and James's father. Tom and Susie's brother. Gill's and Burt's son. Gone but never forgotten in our hearts.

Private family services will be performed the following week.'

The Tobey she knew may have been anywhere between thirty and forty years old, and the timeframe appeared to suit. But where was he now, and why, after five years of living next to him, was he already dead? She comforted herself, "I don't believe in ghosts."

Christina stopped by the public records office on her way to work the following day. She was able to get a copy of the deed of the property next door to hers for a little charge. It revealed that the new neighbour, Patrick, did, in fact, legally own the home, but had just acquired the paperwork one month before. She opened Google Chrome on her phone, perplexed, to check if she could discover earlier property deeds online. She abandoned up after a brief search, overwhelmed by the sheer number of material to go through.

She had plenty of time to contemplate while stacking cans of canned peas on Coles' shelves. Perhaps earlier land records have not yet been digitised? Or maybe she needed a plausible cause to go searching through the past; after all, she had nothing to do with that home legally. Maybe she was simply paranoid, her personal experiences clouding her judgement? However, what was the alternative? Hallucinations caused by medicines combined with alcohol? Is it a genuine, spine-chilling ghost?

She smashed the canisters onto the shelf, laughing hysterically.

Christina saw a little, basic package slipped under her doormat on her way home from work in the early hours of the morning, just before the morning chorus of birds greeted the new day. When she opened the envelope, she found a crumpled piece of paper addressed to her inside. It said:

I'm still alive, but I'm in danger. You, too, are. Tonight at 6 p.m., meet me at Grenwood Park's playground. Come by yourself.

Christina glanced around in terror, but no one was on the street. She couldn't see anybody in either way, not even Mrs Johnsons's tell-tale pulled-back curtain spying on her neighbours. Could this actually be Tom's note? Or was it a ruse?

Christina came ahead of schedule. She sat on the abandoned swing set and started moving her feet in the soil, generating brown dust clouds. Christina decided to quit up after almost an hour of sitting there like a discarded doll. What a scumbag trick, she thought. Christina could feel the late-October cold seeping through her garments, causing the hairs on her arms to stand on edge. She rose up, frustrated and disappointed, and looked for her vehicle keys. She paused as she approached the teeter-totter. In the bushes, there was a movement. Christina pirouetted around, looking for the source of the disturbance in the trees. Christina started marching to her vehicle after hearing no more noises when the flashlight on her phone reflected something in the blackness. Approaching with caution, she saw light reflecting off the shiny surface of a Nike shoe. Following the shoe, she saw a trouser pant and a fleece jacket before her gaze was drawn higher to the person's face. A familiar face, warped by filth and dried blood. Oh my gosh, it's Tom she inhaled. Or, at the very least, what was left of him. Christina sunk to her knees, numb and startled, and started examining his body for signs of life. Maybe it was all a horrible mistake. Or is it a Halloween prank?

A harsh voice from behind her said, "FREEZE."

"Turn slowly around and raise your hands. Christina Wilcock, you are being held in custody for the murder of Tobey Mazokov."

She'd been set up.

CHAPTER TWO

He, Who vanishes

On this particular Thursday evening, it was chilly and windy, but it wasn't just any Thursday. It was Halloween night in Unionville, and it was one of the most widely observed celebrations in the little town. As might be anticipated, the trick-or-treaters were all decked up in their finest and on their way to collect as much candy as they could carry in their bags. Mr. Abby, the one and only neighbourhood parent, was left out of the festivities.

Abby was on his way to pay a visit to an old buddy, Nas, when the incident occurred. The fact that Nas lived on the same street as Mr. Abby meant that the two of them met almost every day to critique one another's yard or to have coffee at one another's home. They were almost best friends, but something occurred on Halloween that caused Mr. Abby to rethink their whole ten-year relationship.

When Abby got to Nas' home, he saw that his vehicle was not to be seen, leading him to speculate as to where Nas had gone on Halloween night knowing that the kids would be lining up around the block to obtain some of his Hershey's and M&M brownies, which he distributed every year. In addition, there was not a single light shining into the home, which caused Abby to become alarmed and concerned. A faint shiver ran down Abby' spine as he made his way up the staircase.

He banged on the door, and it flung open, but Nas was not there to open it. He has been approached by someone, a youngster to be precise, that he has never met before.

"Can you tell me where Nas Diez is?" Mr. Abby said, a perplexed expression on his face.

The tiny child was nowhere to be seen within the home. Suddenly, a woman with red/orange hair arrived from down the corridor, just as Mr. Abby was ready to step inside his home to greet his guests.

"Can I be of assistance?" the woman said as she dried her hands with a dishcloth.

"Where has Nas Diez gone?" Mr. Abby inquired once again.

She stared at him as if he were insane, and said, "Well, Mr. Diez hasn't resided in this home for about 11 years darling," as if he were insane himself. He committed himself in the upstairs bathroom, but I haven't told my children about it yet because I don't want them to believe the home is haunted. "He committed suicide in the upstairs bathroom," the woman murmured in hushed tones as she approached Mr. Abby.

"That can't possibly be the case. 'Only yesterday, Nas and I went out to lunch at the Thin Burger and decided to go watch the new terrifying movie that is screening tonight,' says the author.

She examined Mr. Abby from every angle, as she became more afraid of the seemingly insane guy. Mr. Abby began hammering on the door, yelling, "Don't close that door! " "I'd want to know where my closest buddy has disappeared to!"

He began to get agitated and perplexed, and he lost his cool. After 10 years of friendship with Nas, Abby felt there was no way he could have imagined the events of the previous ten years of his life. He stopped knocking on the door and took a seat on the stairwell's landing. He couldn't think of anything else to do except weep.

This is Mr. Abby' home, he thought, but everything about it, down to the scent of him, seemed to have evaporated as if he had never been there in the first place."

"Please accept my apologies." The sound of a faraway, quiet voice could be heard whispering in the air. Mr. Abby raised his eyes to the ceiling, but there was no one there. "How are you?" he inquired.

As a chilly shudder ran down his spine, nothing but quiet filled the air around him. The anxiousness overtook him as he began going around the yard in front of the house. When he arrived in the backyard, he could immediately see that something was amiss. "Hello?" Mr Abby inquired once again.

As was to be anticipated, there was no response. Mr. Abby turned around to be welcomed by the woman who had entered the home from the other side. Then she smacked him in the face with something hard and heavy, telling him, "I told you there was no one here for you." After he felt the blood draining from his head, Mr. Abby gazed down the barrel of a revolver with distorted vision through his handbag.

a voice that sounded just like Nas Diez said, "The spirit of Nas Diez will never vanish." Yet Mr. Abby is never seen or heard from again when the pistol goes off just as he starts to say anything more.

CHAPTER THREE

I am death

Andrew was finally able to get the confidence to approach the man outdoors. For the last fifteen minutes, he'd been watching him from behind the curtain, wondering why the guy stood there. Had his mother been right when she said he was one of those creeps?

Andrew told the visitor at the edge of their property, "If you're one of those creeps, you'd best scream, man." If not, "I'll fetch my father."

A little nose and thin lips were all that could be seen behind the man's long black hair, which hid the sides of his long, lean face. Those were smiley lips.

As the guy spoke, his voice was quiet and peaceful. 'I am Death,' he said.

With his ginger locks falling over his gloomy face, Andrew tilted his head. At six years old, he was already familiar with the concept of death.

His response was, "You're lying." What happened to your scythe, by the way?" And why don't you cover your head with a hooded black cloak instead? On top of that, you have a head. Bones are all that's left of him."

Andrew was made to feel uneasy by the man's hushed laughter. He hadn't seen this guy before, but this was the first time he'd spoken to him about anything.

Andrew, we live in the current era. In order to seem well, one must dress appropriately."

He tried not to exhibit any signs of anxiety as Andrew's jaw clenched tight. Why are you asking this question, stranger?

"I, Death, am here. Everybody calls me by their first name. All the way down to your mum and dad. As for my appearance, ""

To Andrew's horror, he pulled back the hair on his right cheek to show an especially gruesome scar. There was a lot of red and black tissue, revealing white teeth!

Andrew became terrified as he realised that he was Death. When he got back inside, he called for his parents. When Andrew's shouts drew his father's attention from scrubbing the dishes, he rushed in.

"What's the matter, sir?" he asked. Andrew fought back tears as lavender-scented white foam dripped from his fingertips and into the carpet.

I'm afraid of what awaits me there! There's a hedge right there!"

His father had a puzzled expression on his face. "What?

It was the first time I'd ever spoken to him, and he claimed to be Death. What's more, he remembers my name!

In search of the person or persons responsible for frightening his kid, his father's expression darkened. From a safe distance, Andrew glanced out, but no one was there. Death had gone.

Andrew's father warned him, saying, "You should not laugh about stuff like that." "It's not humorous," he said. He returned to the kitchen with a sour expression on his face.

"But…"

His mother, who was upstairs, said, "What was all the ranting about?"

His father replied, "Nothing," as if nothing had happened. "Andrew is up to his old tricks."

Then there was—

Concern had given way to irritation on his mother's face. There is no excuse for your lack of attire, young guy. "It's fifteen minutes till school begins!"

Honestly, I don't think anybody would believe me. As adults, they could only believe if they saw it for themselves. Andrew grumbled and got dressed for school, despite his reluctance to participate.

Mom dropped Andrew off at school and said, "Have a good day, honey!". If you don't mind waiting for me here till after school, I'll meet you there. I am in awe of you!

Andrew couldn't stop thinking about his brush with Death during the first period of school. It seemed to him that he was acting like a kid when he ran away from the situation so quickly. To be sure he wasn't simply another creep, he should have tested Death. The next time I meet him, I'll put him to the test.

Please join us in the classroom. "Andrew, would you mind joining us?"

Andrew despised the guy who had that voice as much as he despised the overtones. Miss Astra. The instructor.

A trip to the world of fairies once again, I suppose?

For some reason, she opted to target Andrew anytime he was prone to daydreaming during class. She had the most awful voice in the world. He wasn't daydreaming today, however. He was pondering the end of everything.

Andrew had already forgotten about Death by the time the bells rung for lunch, with hunger taking precedence over everything else. He didn't see the guy claiming to be

Death again until after lunch, when he stood on the edge of the playing field and stared directly at him.

A shiver ran down Andrew's spine, and his natural inclination was to flee the campus. However, he later came to regret his choice and approached the unknown individual.

Tensely asking, "What are you doing here?" he tried not to tremble as he spoke.

It was Andrew who was targeted this time. The towering guy stared him down. Using one hand, he grasped the fence bar like a scythe. It's "to kill you"

Andrew's hair stood on end. In spite of this, he didn't flee.

Screaming was the last thing on his mind. In the event that you attempt to harm me, "I will scream and the instructors will arrive."

Despite the man's small lips and lengthy hair, the terrible scar was clearly visible. Andrew's tummy started to rumble as he ate his meal.

This is your moment," the guy said, without rushing. There is nothing that can be done to stop it.

Andrew's words was moving quicker than his heart as he demanded, "Prove it first." "I'll go with you if you can prove to me that you are Death." Denying Death made no sense, right? This is something he was prepared for, having watched the movies.

This time, the man's gleaming teeth were on display. "You've got a lot going for you, child. It's going well. "How am I going to prove it to you?"

Andrew pondered this. Is there a way to verify that you are death? Of course, by committing mass murder! Did he genuinely wish to cause the death of another person? He wasn't a fan of the concept. If the individual was terrible, he thought it would be okay...

Finally saying, "Here's what I want you to do," he explained his instructions. "If you pass these three exams, I'll give you my life." For the sake of time, he said three.

"What is the first one?" Death inquired without hesitation.

Andrew gulped it down. "Our neighbourhood is plagued by a vicious dog. When I was a little child, he bit me, and I want you to get rid of him now that I'm older. Because he barks at me whenever I go by, I don't like him."

Death smirked once again, showing the hideous scars on his face. If you insist, Andrew, I'll play along. But you have to promise me something. You'll be there if I win. Deal?"

"And what if you lose?"

Once that is decided, I'll leave you in the hands of your higher power. If you want my life, then you can have it. The cops are at your disposal, if you so want.

Andrew agreed since he thought it was fair. Death remained standing there, observing Andrew until the last school bell rung. Andrew returned inside the school, looking back at Death as he did so.

Andrew waited for his mother to pick him up after school. He continued scanning the room to see whether Death was lurking behind a corner, but he couldn't see the ominous figure. That dog must have gotten away from him.

His mother showed there, and the two of them proceeded to the store to get some items that his mother really needed. His favourite thing about shopping was pushing the shopping cart, and he was preoccupied with thoughts of death while he went about his business. Is it truly time for him to leave this world? But he was just a child...

The lady who lived a few homes down the street from them was one of Mom's acquaintances. Since she'd just heard terrible news, she seemed anxious.

What's wrong, Brenda? Andrew's mother inquired, "You don't look too well."

He just phoned me," I said. "Oh, Roberd. "Our puppy was hit by a car! Help!

As she hurriedly exited the shop, we might assume she was on her way home. Andrew's pupils dilated. It was a hit! Brenda was the owner of the dog that had attacked Andrew in the past. He had been murdered by death!

Mom was taken aback by his attitude of disbelief. My sweetheart, don't worry about it, you know. I'm certain that the dog will be okay, however. When you play on the street, I'd want to see you be a little more cautious from now on, okay?"

Mom, the dog isn't going to be OK, Andrew thought as he nodded. Death has been tasked with putting an end to his life on my orders.

He was taken aback by how swiftly it all transpired. For the second exam, he'll have to come up with a solution quickly to avoid failing.

Death arrived under Andrew's window as he leaned on the ledge of his room later that evening. It wasn't until nobody was watching that Andrew saw the slim form of a guy stand on the sidewalk, waiting for the right moment to vault over the fence and into Andrew's home. When Andrew finally opened the window, he waited patiently for them to talk.

The man's voice sounded like silk as he said, "I completed your first exam."

Andrew broke the news that the dog was dead. He heard his neighbours grumbling about a hit-and-run incident. If it wasn't you, how could you have known?

The guy took a breather. Is there anything more you'd want to see?

Andrew's face was red with embarrassment. His head was shaken, and some of the curls fell into his eyes as he shook it back and forth. Once he tried to play with a dead squirrel by poking it with his finger. It had a terrible odour.

'Name your second test, youngster.' Death instructed. The warm-up is beneficial. Do you have a plan for when I'll kill you?

Andrew's mouth clenched. For a few hours, he contemplated who Death should target next. The task of raising a dog was simple and anybody could do it. He may be hit by a passing vehicle by accident. The next exam should be more difficult.

He hesitated before saying, "Mr. Rogers." What do I want you to do with his body? "That dog might have been struck by anybody."

As the saying goes, "Who is Mr. Rogers, child?"

Andrew squinted his eyes. Then why didn't you know about everyone?

One of the men in the room pushed back his hair to reveal a scar: "There are many Rogers in the world, youngster." In order to tell them apart, it's "quite difficult."

Despite his initial hesitance, Andrew pointed in the direction of the neighbor's home. "It's the neighboring elderly man." In general, I find him to be a quite unpleasant person, especially when it comes to playing outside in front of his home with my friends. On top of that, he's now unwell, coughing uncontrollably at night, so he should be on your list already."

It was Death who made the lightest of chuckles. "I see," I respond. "He's a whiz." He took a breather. Please inform me about the third exam. This evening, I'm in the mood to get some work done.

Andrew took a deep breath and forced himself to swallow. He spent a lot of time contemplating the third aim. It was she whom he detested the most.

He was scared someone might hear him say, "Miss Astra." "Me and my high school English instructor. "She's a bully."

As the black-haired guy grinned and nodded, Andrew's neck was tingling with fear and excitement. Turned around and returned the way he came after making sure no one was looking. People avoided staring at him as he walked down the street. After a while, Andrew became persuaded that this guy was in fact the deity of death.

However, he wasn't certain just yet.

He'll probably find out tomorrow.

Andrew's mother told him at breakfast that Mr. Rogers had died peacefully the night before. Andrew sat at the table, still half sleepy, eating on bread and jam while he slept off. He had nightmares of people dying all around him last night, and he couldn't sleep at all. He was surprised by the news, even though he had expected it.

His father had a cup of coffee. He described the individual as "extremely unwell." "I suppose it was time for him to go. You see, Andrew, as individuals age, they are more susceptible to being ill and passing away quietly. Then then, you don't have to worry about it, since your time isn't coming any time soon. He put on a jovial face in an attempt to cheer things up.

When I smiled back, Andrew's grin was a false one. On the inside, he was aware that his time was running out. Death has already passed two of his examinations. Now, all that was left was Miss Astra. A new academic year would shortly begin.

Before Rogers' death, the dog was hit by a car.... 'God bless you both,'" they say. Andrew felt a little sorry for his mother, who was clearly distressed by all of this. When he died, he worried how she would respond.

Then Andrew went to school, even though he couldn't bring himself to eat anything. Andrew's mother dropped him off at school as usual, and he went up the school steps with an awful sensation of suspense increasing with each step. Is Miss Astra going to be in the classroom today or tomorrow? Alternatively, was she already deceased?

Because of his fear, he hesitated to attend the classroom. Then then, he didn't want to seem like a moron waiting outside the door. The rest of the students were already waiting for the instructor to arrive, and they were all conversing happily.

Andrew's heart was pounding as he sat at his desk. He prayed for Miss Astra's well-being, realising that he had done so. He didn't think he could pull it off.

The clock struck 8 and the school bell sounded, signalling the beginning of the first class session.

There was no instructor present. Andrew's tummy began to rumble. Others poked Andrew and inquired as to what was making him so nervous. In spite of their pleas, Andrew continued to stare at the entrance, hoping that Miss Astra would finally arrive. He hoped Death didn't exist and that he still had time to live.

As if on cue, the door burst open.

Andrew's heart had stopped.

In fact, it wasn't even Miss Astra who was responsible for the murder.

Instead, Mr. Peterson, the replacement instructor, was the culprit. And he didn't seem to be in the best of spirits.

A low voice and bowed shoulders were all that he could do to greet the class, "Good morning."

"Oh no," I'm so sorry.

A sad piece of information has come to light for me. This morning, Miss Astra, your normal teacher, was involved in a horrific accident.

Andrew couldn't bear it any longer and decided to quit. It seemed to him that if he remained there for much longer, his heart would explode. His sudden exit from the classroom elicited gasps and puzzled stares from the students around him.

After leaving the building, he hurried to the nearby playground, his eyes welling up with tears and his breathing laboured. Death was a genuine possibility. In addition to killing a dog, he shot and murdered two persons. He was about to be taken away by Death. Despite Andrew's best efforts, he was able to keep the meal down. Inhaling deeply, he rested his chin on the basketball pole.

"Your exams are over, youngster," whispered a soothing voice, and when Andrew looked around, there he was. When you see him, you won't believe your eyes. The glass shards on his coat and the bruise on his forehead both looked suspicious, but Andrew was too shaken to notice.

"So you truly are Death," he said, his voice trembling. It was no longer a game to him; he was exhausted and lonely.

As Death said, "I told you so." "Andrew, hurry up. In the end, I came out on top. "You must accompany me," I said.

Andrew's eyes welled up with tears as he imagined his parents' reactions if they learnt of his death. When they find out, do you think they'll be sad?

That's OK with me," Andrew agreed. Death could not be argued with. For him, there was no doubt about it.

He grinned and received a helping hand from Death. Andrew accepted it reluctantly.

Just before Mr. Peterson came out looking for him, they departed the school playground.

Decorah, Iowa, was rocked by the news a few days later. One of America's most notorious serial killers, Walt Nick, 45 years old, has taken another victim, this time a 6-year-old kid. According to a press release from the police, they've been pursuing this individual throughout seven states for the last five years. It's been stated that he's always been interested in boys between the ages of 4 and 9. Despite the fact that this was the first time the psychopath had killed two persons, one of them was a teacher who was killed in a vehicle accident and the other who was a senior citizen who was choked to death in his sleep.

The most perplexing aspect of the case for the police was the fact that all of the victims seemed to have deliberately travelled to the murder location with the perpetrator. There was never a hint of an uphill battle.

They looked like victims of some cruel prank that the murderer perpetrated on them, and the kids fell for it because they're kids.

CHAPTER FOUR

I'm Becoming Insane

It was a mistake for me to come. After getting into this taxi cab and driving all the way across town to get here, I should have known better than to do so. Nonetheless, I did. When I saw that face among hundreds of others, I wondered whether it was just my mind playing tricks on me. At first, I wondered whether it was some kind of optical illusion, or maybe a nasty prank.

I considered it possible that it was a sign that I needed to get out of the house. Take a few sips of anything to drink. Or two, or three.

Is it possible that I'm becoming insane?

Their image may be seen everywhere. I'm not familiar with them. I wondered whether they were familiar with me. But those violet eyes, with that nefarious scar... That blood, pouring out of their nostrils, Can you imagine how I may have met them previously and not remembered it?

Is it possible that I'm becoming insane?

When I initially spotted them, I assumed they could be in need of some assistance. I had to push my way through a sea of fleshy bodies on the pavement to get to them, but by the time I did, they were already vanished. A spatter of blood was the only thing that had taken their place. Two or three drips, maybe three, of water trickling down the concrete.

I didn't give it any consideration at all. Just a feeling of regret. I was disappointed that I couldn't assist them. I've also been able to assist others. "Katrina, stop assisting other people and take a moment to think about yourself," my mother often tells me. But why should I be concerned about myself? There's nothing more I can do for myself at this point.

Is it possible that I'm becoming insane?

I wonder whether I would have forgotten about the ribbed skin and the burns that specked those hands. If I hadn't run across them again, I may have decided to go on. It's the same road. I'm on my way to the office. And, once again, by the time I got to them, there was nothing left. Some blood splatters on the New York streets, combining with the muck and dirt of the sidewalks.

My buddy, who was with me at the time, grabbed my arm and said, "Katrina, you're looking a little pale. Is everything well with you?"

"Didn't you happen to notice them?" I questioned her, but I couldn't look her in the eyes. I was preoccupied with searching among the throngs of people for that caramel skin. That dreadful cut across the bridge of their nose.

"Who? Katrina, your hands are trembling. Is it necessary for you to take a seat?"

Was it necessary for me to take a seat? Is it possible that I was trembling? I didn't know what to say. I don't remember precisely what occurred, but I do recall that I ended up at my place of employment. Somehow.

Is it possible that I'm becoming insane?

A significant difference existed between the third time and the previous two. Maybe it's not that different after all. It took place along the same length of sidewalk as before. In front of the same McDonald's that has been shuttered for years with no sign of a replacement for the squalid shack.

However, it was different in that there were just a few individuals there. In New York, this is unusual for the middle of the day. It was only myself and a few stragglers who'd managed to skip the lunch rush as well. The throng was small, and this time when I noticed them, I was certain that it wasn't a trick of the light this time around. It was not a ruse to take advantage of the large number of people.

I panicked as soon as I saw them and said, "Hold on a minute! Please!"

The heads in the vicinity of me turned. Theirs, however, did not. My breathing became more rapid, almost wildly, and my pace became a jog. It's a sprint. They, too, took to the streets. Almost as quick as I am, which is saying a lot considering how fast I am. Having ran since I can remember, I've won a slew of track and field championships along the way. Medals. I was certain that I would be able to catch up to them despite the fact that they were twice as quick as I was.

"Please! What is your name?"

It seemed like they were about to round a corner, and by the time I got there, their regular calling card was splattered at my feet. And what about them? Gone. The hustling and bustling had taken over.

I knelt near the pool of blood, my breathing laboured. I ran my fingers through it, almost as if I were attempting to grab at it without thinking.

"Is it true that you're bleeding?" When a compassionate lady placed a hand on my back, it was so soft that it made me jump, I slapped her hand away. She took a few steps back, her palm clasped to her breast in horror.

"I'm sorry..." I managed as I wiped the blood from my jeans with my hand. Taking a step back. "Am I going out of my mind?" I wonder aloud.

Was it really me? Is it possible that I was suffering from a mental illness?

So that's how I landed myself here in the first place. When the phone rang, and my friend's cheerful voice boomed through it, "Katrina, I got us into this party!" I burst out laughing. After all, who was I to say that I couldn't attend? So that's what I did. Maybe I simply wanted to go away. Perhaps work was becoming an excessive source of stress.

I knew as soon as I went inside the bar that I shouldn't have done it. They were in attendance. And, after all, why wouldn't they? Hadn't they been following me around, watching me?

But just on that particular stretch of road, the one that passes by the old McDonald's. I'd never seen anything like them before. It was the first and only time I'd ever seen them somewhere else in all three of my encounters with them. Yet, here they were, perched on a bar stool at the end of the night, swirling a drink with a blue-tinged finger as if they'd been there their whole lives.

The environment altered around them, and they were almost completely unaware of their existence. To that metal, which protrudes from their stomach. To the dark circles that ring the drooping corners of their eyes. Perhaps they weren't blind after all, for they were strolling by them, speaking joyfully and laughing. Perhaps they didn't perceive anything wrong with it since they were blind to it.

Is it possible that I'm becoming insane?

My buddy grabbed my arm and steered me toward a table, her head swaying in time with the music. In the same manner that the metal would bounce in their stomachs with every sip of their beverage.

"Come on," she said, giggling. "There's someone I'd want you to get to know."

I murmured, as I wiggled out of her clutches, "Hold on a minute. I... I feel the desire to go to the restroom. All right, I'll be right back, all right?"

She shrugged her shoulders. "Okay, Katrina, but don't take too long. We didn't go all the way across town just so you could go to the bathroom."

The woman pushed by me, and I made my way toward the individual behind the counter. This time, as they took off, I was prepared, having already begun running. The walkway is already being torn up in their wake.

Perhaps a part of me knew I'd never be able to keep up with them on foot. Perhaps I realised, if reluctantly, that they were at least as quick as I was, and that even with their foot head-start, it was still too much for me to handle.

I saw a guy dismounting from his motorbike. The colour of their stomach metal is green, which matches the colour of their skin. He was preoccupied in a conversation with a young lady. Alternatively, two or three. I've never cared for a player, particularly when I could see the ring glinting on his left hand, so I took advantage of the situation and snatched the ring. He had mounted it and went about halfway down the road when he discovered it was no longer there.

Is it possible that I'm becoming insane?

They were still in sight, sprinting down the street, and I accelerated the bike to keep up with them. In the same way that I'd never rode a horse before, I'd also never stolen anything before.

While the figure maintained a steady pace, I did not, and we had been at it for many adrenaline-pumping minutes when I realised that we had managed to return to that particular street somehow. That was the first time I'd seen them on that particular street. This is the second time. The third is the most important.

When I was about to say anything, they walked into the road just as I was thinking about it. It was there in front of me. I swerved out of the way, terrified. That's how I came to be in this situation. The tyres of the motorcycle skidded under the control of an unskilled rider.

The bike squeals as it slides to the left on the road, but they don't move despite the noise. When I scream, a ratchet mechanism burns the interior of my throat. "Get out of the way!" yells the boss.

Despite this, they remain.

The bike slips under me, and I grab for whatever traction I can find in the hopes of reversing the situation. Regret flashes before my eyes at the same rate as the glaring headlights of a speeding automobile. I shouldn't have come here in the first place.

After being struck by the automobile, which drives the motorbike into my abdomen, I cry out loud. Pain eats away at me like a red-hot flame, and as I'm flung against the stairs of that old McDonald's, I see that my nose has began to bleed, which I find amusing. The rain is splattering down on the pavement. The blood was dripping from the side of the green metal poking out of my stomach.

Is it possible that I'm becoming insane?

I have tears streaming down the side of my face from my violet eyes, warm tears that are running down the scar on my cheek. In track, there was a hurdle that I missed. After wiping them away, I see that the motorbike in front of me is on fire for the first time. The flames have licked my hands, searing them, yet I don't seem to be aware of the discomfort.

Despite the fact that I have a deep cut going down the middle of my forehead, I don't experience the anguish that should be there. As I glance about me, I can see a dirty reflection in one of the half-shattered McDonald's windows, among the shouts of the sirens, the smoke and flames, and the pleas for help.

I'm aware of them. I beg you, I beg you, right there and rasping, "What is your name? Please let me know."

Despite this, I am certain that they will not respond. What would be the point of doing so? I'm already aware of this.

One question, though, remains unanswered. One that is crystal obvious despite my jumbled state of mind.

Is it possible that I'm becoming insane?

CHAPTER FIVE

I'm going to let go

I am surrounded by frigid walls and a rough seat. The only light that could enter the box isn't, and it's doing it in a clever way because of the dampness. My mobile phone is ringing with an icy voice, but I can no longer hear it.

I understand what it's saying. How could I have forgotten?

As a child, I imagined a time machine that would allow me to go back and forth in time. The leather shoes chafe on my ankles where my rushed preparation left it folded at the top. I feel my feet as they stroll. My turtleneck's hem was likewise tucked into my body, but it was deliberate. The care I took with my shoes now seems inconsequential, but then I wished I had remembered. On the way to Mr. Mason's home, I was still buckling my belt. This was the first time I'd seen him in a long time, and I had certain things I wanted to tell him. On October 30th, he'd been very mean to me, and I'd finally come up with a few responses while taking a shower.

Instead of walking into the room and saying, "Hey old man! Wouldn't you appreciate it if I simply left your shrubs alone?" Nobody cares enough about you to take care of your grass, wouldn't you? Maybe I might instruct the youngsters to stop coming to shovel your driveway and start shovelling mine instead.. After all, I'm a grown-up now, and it's time for me to stop behaving like a child. I may have to go through with it. You'll understand why in a moment. Due to the fact that my only desire is for you to die in this home. To avoid sliding and shattering a fragile old bone, I hope you never go out in the cold without freezing your hands and feet. It's my prayer that you perish this winter since you don't want my aid! There is no doubt in your mind that you are capable of maintaining your own yard! I hope you're having a great day! In addition, I wish you all the best for the funeral."

I wish I hadn't ever considered uttering those words, much less been ready to do so. I was 10 years too late, anyhow. You'd think I would have checked the obituaries after thinking about it for so long, but I didn't.

Immediately as my icy finger hit the chipped plastic button, I realised that something was amiss with the doorbell. Puffy, Mr. Mason's dog, should have sounded an alarm. She should have yelled loud enough to alert the whole neighbourhood that Mr. Mason had arrived.

I was surprised when the small girl opened the door and shouted out for her father. I could still smell the scent of dish soap on his dish towel as he walked through the door. When he asked if I had anything he could need, I responded no, then he asked if I knew him. Despite my reluctance to inquire, he broke the stalemate by asking me what I was doing there. Because Mr. Mason wasn't in the room, I almost choked as the words I'd practised for years ripped themselves out of my throat to kill him. When I finally spoke, my voice was stiff and loud, despite my best efforts to keep it quiet. He gazed at me in disbelief, and I felt the weight of shame on my conscience.

'Mr. Mason is no longer a part of our family,' he added. My body trembled as he went on, and my perplexity must have shown through. "He passed away on October 30th, 2009, 10 years ago."

That night, I had pruned his shrubs, and I felt a twinge of remorse. His dog and his owner were poisoned the same night I warned him of my plans. What happened to Puffy? My guilt would be cleansed if I could simply see Puffy. It would have simply been a terribly opportune moment. Knowing that it was better to not know how they died or whether they had both died was enough to keep me from asking, but knowing that the weight of ignorance and possible guilt was lighter than the guilt that would come from knowing. As a result, I felt a stirring inside me that went much deeper than my heart, conscience, and soul. I was certain that I had murdered them. I was to blame for what happened here.

When I desired bad things for someone, bad things happened. I confessed to Mr. Mason's son that I had slain his father, and he accepted my apology. While the daughter was standing there, bewildered by what a stranger was saying about her grandfather's death, I confessed to the crime. A broken bird or an old weak dog that barked to keep her partly deaf owner safe, I surrendered myself to their compassion like a broken bird or an old weak dog. Confessions of my sins poured out of me, and I begged them to take my life and toss it into the abyss.

The tears are still pouring down my face, and I can still feel the heat rising up my cheeks. Tears that ripped me away from everything and everyone I had ever known. I pled guilty to avoid going through the ordeal of going to court. I felt the harsh, crazy, and life-consuming remarks spill out in front of everyone.

In my haste and impulsiveness, I behaved as if I were a crazed person. Possibly I was, or still am, a crazy person, as the case may be. Because of my weak conscience, I've spent my whole life in a prison cell with nothing to do and a lot of time wasted. Perhaps I'd rather die than live.

"Are you ready to die?" is the question. It's as if I'm living in a perpetual echo chamber. I'd want to say yes, but I need to hear the rest of what it has to say first.

"It wasn't his fault; it was yours. Please return home. Let yourself go and forget what you've done to yourself."

I'm going to let go...